My Annoying Mom

Author:
Tayyaba Amir

MY ANNOYING MOM

Copyright © Tayyaba Amir - 2019
All rights reserved. Printed in Pakistan. No part of this book may be used or reproduced in any manner whatsoever without written permission except in the case of brief quotations embodied in critical articles or reviews.
This book is a work of fiction. Names, characters, businesses, organizations, places, events and incidents either are the product of the author's imagination or are used fictitiously. Any resemblance to actual persons, living or dead, events, or locales is entirely coincidental.

Book and Cover Design by Thazbook Designs.
ISBN: 978-969-7851-08-9
First Edition: September 2019
Second Edition: November 2019
Third Edition: June 2024
Printed By: Thazbook Publications.
www.thazbook.com info@thazbook.com
avaiable at: https://www.facebook.com/AuthorTayyabaAmir/

Contents

Chapter 1   A Dream --------------------------------5

Chapter 2   Meet My Dad --------------------------16

Chapter 3   My Annoying Mom -------------------28

Chapter 4   The Outings ---------------------------35

Chapter 5   Consistent Problems-------------------47

Chapter 6   A Fight---------------------------------55

Chapter 7   An Accident----------------------------63

Chapter 8   An Angel-------------------------------71

To My Kids

Chapter 1
A dream

The school assembly ground was buzzing with bright-faced boys and girls. The kindergartners, full of energy, stood at the front of the stage, which was situated at the narrow end of the rectangular ground. Behind them, the primary and secondary class students, neatly dressed in their uniforms, were lined up in queues according to their grades, waiting for the assembly to begin.

A middle-aged teacher on the stage wore glasses on the end of her nose. She gazed at the pile of pages in her right hand, then brought the pages closer to see the names more clearly. As each page came into focus, she lifted the microphone in her hand and clearly announced the names for everyone to hear. These were the names of successful pupils for the annual prize distribution. When each name was announced, a child would come forward from their row, walk to the stage, and receive a shield and congratulations from the headmistress. Meanwhile, a cameraman captured the proud moment, which made an enjoyable memory for the student.

After a pause, the teacher announced, "Student of the Year award goes to Shoaib Ahmed, grade 5."

Amidst thunderous applause, I walked proudly towards the stage, my chin held high and a beaming smile on my face. I stood before the headmistress, gazed directly into her eyes, and bowed respectfully. Then, I raised my hands to receive the award shield.

The sun suddenly became enormously brighter and I covered my eyes with my hands as the beaming light made it impossible to see. While shielding my eyes with my hand, I tried to open them slightly and struggled to know the reason for this sudden hindrance. Meanwhile, I struggled to recognise a female voice too, calling my name. It seemed familiar, but unidentifiable. All of a sudden, the applause faded, and I opened my eyes slightly.

"Shobi! Shobi! Wake up, sweetie. Shobi, you are late for school."

"It's no one but my mom," I murmured, opened my eyes and sat up on the wrinkled bed.

The bright light that interrupted my dream came from the unveiled windows.

"Mom! Why did you wake me up at the last moment? Couldn't you wait for a while?" Annoyingly I said.

She paused and stared blankly at me with her big brown eyes. She was wearing a light blue scarf around her face, which suited her wheatish complexion. The scarf covered her brown hair completely.

"In my dream, I was just about to receive my Student of the Year award from my headmistress," I added.

"Shobi, hurry up! Otherwise, instead of an award, you will get a punishment."

I reluctantly got out of bed and headed to the bathroom. As I washed my face, my eyes started to hurt and I made a hissing sound because it hurt so much! I knew I shouldn't have stayed up late reading my new book. Mom had told me to go to bed on time, but I just couldn't stop reading my adventure book. It was so exciting! I kept turning the pages until I finished the whole book, and it was already 11:30 PM!

Usually, I listened to Mom when she called me, but sometimes this used to clash with my inner desires. When I was younger, everyone praised me for being well-behaved, and I even got a special certificate at school for being good. But then a new girl named Sana joined my class, and she became the teachers' favorite. I wondered why she got the certificate every year, even though I was better at things like volleyball and chess. She was shorter than me and couldn't even beat me in a game! I wished my dream that morning would come true, because I was the tallest and smartest boy in my class. My grandma said my big, shiny eyes showed how wise I was, and they went well with my light brown skin and strong face. She also said I looked just like my dad, which made me happy.

My five year old sister Sarah greeted me at the dinner table with a big smile. She always smiled a lot, just like the Cheshire Cat in Alice in Wonderland! Sarah had a round face, dark brown eyes, braided brown hair, and a tiny nose that pointed upwards. Everyone adored her because she was cute, but no one knew that she was actually a rabble router with rosy cheeks.

"Good morning, brother."

"Morning," I replied scornfully and dragged a chair to the table, making a scratching sound on the floor.

"Shobi, don't drag the chair like that," Mom scolded me while serving breakfast.

"Please, Mom! Don't call me Shobi," I protested and picked up my glass of milk.

"Sweetheart, you don't remember how much you

loved that name when you were this little," Mom said with a warm smile, holding her hand up to show how small I used to be. Then, she gave me a gentle kiss.

"Now I don't," I replied with a snort. "Because you call me Shobi, everyone at school has started teasing me about it." I shuddered, remembering the incident from a couple of days ago, which played out in my mind like a scary movie.

It was home time. All the students, eager to get home as soon as possible, were waiting to be dismissed. Some were still neatly dressed, but most looked like they had come from a wrestling match. One was missing his tie and another his badge. Several boys had their shirts out of their pants, and a few girls stood slack with loose hair and dirty shoes. A few kids even had tomato ketchup stains on their light blue shirts. Everyone chattered continuously. Tired teachers were trying hard to discipline them. Parents were entering the ground, searching for their children, and managing to escape with them from the crowded ground.

Mom, followed by other parents, came to look for me, but I was busy talking with my best friend, Abdul Rehman, about the latest video game launched a few days ago, and the most interesting part was that his father agreed to buy one for him. I did not see Mom waving at me, nor heard the teacher calling my name.

Suddenly, to my intense embarrassment, I heard Mom yell out, "Shobi! Shobi! Come here."

By the time I turned, she had already called me several times. I looked around and prayed to Allah that no one realised it was my name, but my classmates were not fooled. Asad put his finger on the tip of the nose, moved his head back and forth, and cried out, "Shobi baby, your mom is calling you!" Rest of them chuckled and exchanged high-fives. I sprinted off and didn't look back but their mocking remarks chased me till my exit from school.

My face was as red as a hot chilli and I argued with Mom in the car on the way home. "Why did you have to call me Shobi in front of everybody? I was dying with embarrassment."

"Oh dear, I am really sorry, sweetie. I didn't mean any harm," she explained. "You couldn't hear you teachers, so I just tried—"

"My useless classmates will now make fun of me," I said, feeling miserable. From that day, Asad and his gang never missed a chance to bully me.

Sarah's voice brought me back from this horrible memory as she triumphantly showed her empty plate to Mom, "Mom, I have finished my toast."

While Mom appreciated her I grunted, "If Asad calls me Shobi again and makes fun of me, I will teach him a lesson," I told her.

"No, sweetheart. A fight is not a solution to any problem."

I put the empty glass on the table and picked up my bag.

"Finish your toast, sweetie," Mom reminded me.

"I'm full, Mom," I replied, but as usual, she didn't listen and handed the toast to me. "You can eat it on the way."

She picked up the car keys and Sarah's school bag and headed outside. We settled into our small blue Mehran and she drove us to school. She tried to cheer me up while driving, but I was lost in my thoughts, gazing at the cars running on the road and nibbling my toast.

From that day on, I started hating my nickname. Every time someone called me Shobi, I felt like cringing. I wished I had a cool nickname like my friends, something that wouldn't make me feel like I wanted to hide under a rock. And to make things worse, I was starting to think that good things just didn't happen to me very often. I was ten years old and already felt like I was having a tough time. It seemed like everything was going wrong, and I was stuck with a nickname that I couldn't stand!"

Well, it was just my day. My lucky younger sister always presented herself nicely. Mom and Dad always adored her more than me, and I couldn't help but feel like I was stuck in her shadow. I had to admit, I wasn't too fond of her at the moment. Mom would often say that my grumpy mood was making me think crazy thoughts, and that my wishes were always coming true - but I didn't see how that was possible when everything seemed to be going so wrong!"

Ugh…seriously, I never understood Mom. She was always making a big deal out of everything! Mom would exaggerate so much that I would roll my eyes and think, "Really, Mom? That's not how it happened at all! However, I must say, Dad was pretty cool. He usually got me what I wanted, like that awesome pair of Nike shoes, a Puma T-shirt, and some other sweet sports gear. But, there was one thing he hadn't gotten me yet - that super cool smartwatch I had been begging for!

I walked into class feeling pretty low, but things got worse when I saw Asad flaunting his brand new smartwatch to a bunch of boys.

"He must've found some secret feature," I muttered to myself.

One of the boys was totally drooling over it, saying, "Wow, Asad, that's so cool! It must've cost a fortune!"

Asad just smiled and said, "Yeah, it's really expensive."

I rolled my eyes and whispered to Abdul Rehman, "He's always showing off, and his friends follow him like little ducklings. I wish I could show him who's boss!" Abdul Rehman giggled, and I talked to myself, "When I get my own smartwatch, everyone will forget about his boring stuff!"

After school, as soon as I reached home, I dumped my bag on the floor, changed into comfy clothes, and hurried to the dining table for lunch. Just as I sat down, Mom emerged from the kitchen with a warm smile and said, "Great, that was quick! I just finished giving Sarah a bath."

I reminded her, "Mom, you promised I could play games on my tablet after lunch!"

She replied sweetly, "Of course, dear, but first, finish your veggies."

I groaned and gazed at the unappetizing vegetables. "Ugh, veggies again? We had them just a few days ago!"

Mom chuckled and said, "Actually, sweetie, that was a week ago, and those were different veggies."

I muttered under my breath, "I have to suffer through this to play my games..."

I loved playing video games after school and couldn't understand why Mom didn't get it that it was so much fun. I forced down the veggies and quickly finished my meal, eager to start my gaming session.

Besides video games, my favorite part of the day was the evening. I had a crew of friends who lived just around the corner, and we'd play cricket till the streetlights came on. I was the star batsman and bowler, and nothing beat the thrill of taking the last wicket. But she always insisted, "No matter how much of the match is left, you have to be at home before the sun sets."

In my mind, I was the smart one who knew what was best for me, but Mom always seemed to dictate me — and that really annoyed me.

Chapter 2
A Meet My Dad

In the classroom, Miss Tania, a tall and slender woman with a kind face, stood beside the whiteboard, marker in hand. Her long hair settled down her neck, and she wore her signature outfit - a dark shirt paired with light-colored trousers. She meticulously wrote detailed instructions for the essay titled 'Meet my Dad' on the board, and the students silently copied them down.

At the end of the lecture, she asked me to erase the board, and as I stood up, Asad whispered, "Shobi baby, your teacher is calling."

My face flushed with embarrassment, but Miss

Tania overheard him and swiftly called him out. "Asad, come here and repeat what you just said," she said, pointing a firm finger at him. Despite her friendly appearance, she didn't tolerate bullying in her class, and Asad was about to face the consequences of his taunt. With the slowest steps ever, Asad made his way to the front of the class and apologized, much to my delight. Miss Tania had a soft spot for me, and it was no secret - she admired my knowledge of her subject and often praised my insights.

"You all will write this essay at home," Miss Tania announced. "Three students with the most comprehensive essay will read it aloud in front of the whole class." She collected her stuff from the table and left.

Like everyone else, the announcement excited me, and I thought all day about what to write about my dad. Finally, I started to gather my thoughts on my way home.

'My dad is a man like no other. He is tall and handsome, with a dark brown beard that I think makes him even more handsome. He has a broad face, dark brown eyes, and thick eyebrows. He loves me a lot and wants to make us all happy, but my mom always interferes. Whenever I ask for a new toy, she forbids him from buying it, and explains that I had a new one a few days ago. Because Dad adores her, he nods at whatever she says and smiles. He often says that Mom is his queen. We hardly meet on weekdays because of the nature of his job. He works from nine in the morning to eleven at night, but we spend weekends together with outings to malls and amusement parks or any place I choose. He comes to my school functions and never forgets to reward me for my performance, whether curricular or extracurricular. Recently, I won a debate competition at school, and, obviously, I deserve a present. I am desperately waiting for the weekend to meet my dad and ask for my reward.

The ideas were swarming in my brain like a bunch of busy bees! I was on a mission to capture them all in my notebook, but it was a tough job! I was halfway done with my essay when... "Hey, come out and play!" my friends yelled from outside my window! It was like a magic spell that made me drop my pen and run to join the fun! Who needs writing when adventure is calling? We had planned an epic cycling adventure the day before, and I was super excited. Every other evening, we'd ride our bikes around our building, feeling the wind in our hair and the sun on our faces.

When I asked Mom to go, she warned, "You will not leave until your homework is done."

"I don't know why Mom keeps pushing me to do my homework. What if it is not done for a day or two?

Would aliens come and imprison me? Obviously not, Mom. Why are you so worried about my homework?" My mind was a whirlwind of thoughts.

I hurriedly wrote just to fill the page. As soon as I finished, I shut the notebook, stuffed it in my bag, and swiftly escaped from Mom's prison.

"Hey, Shoaib! What took you so long?" My friend Usama called out as I came out of the house.

"Homework!" I sighed

He turned his bicycle and pedalled off. Sunlight radiated from a brilliant blue sky, broken by scattered white wisps. I took a deep breath, relishing the cool breeze, and swiftly pedalled to follow him. Three other boys of our small gang joined us at the end of the street. We enjoyed racing, and everyone tried to outdo each other.

At the nearby park, a few older boys were enthusiastically playing cricket. Their shouts and cheers filled the air with life. We pedalled faster and weaved among them to cross the park. I was the last rider in the queue, and as I followed my friends, one of the big boys grabbed the handlebar of my bicycle. I stopped with a jolt and leaned back to stop myself from falling. Astonished, I gazed into his big eyes, but his unfriendly stare warned me not to say anything. He pointed a finger at me and said in a level voice, "Don't disturb us again," and released my bike. I quickly rejoined my friends.

"What happened, Shoaib? Why did he stop you?" Usman asked.

"They think they own the park," I said, fuming with anger. "I'll teach them a lesson as soon as I get a chance."

None of us enjoyed the ride after that, and we

returned home.

On the last day of school week, I headed to the lounge after dinner and took my seat in front of the TV. "Mom, I will not go to bed until Dad comes home." I announced.

"Sweetheart, he will be late. You should go to your room and sleep, You can see him tomorrow morning."

"Please, Mom! Let me stay up," I begged her. She smiled and had to agree.

Suddenly, Sarah appeared from nowhere, grabbed the TV remote controller, and ran off with a giggle. I imidiately ran after her to get it back. I had been waiting the whole week for my favourite TV show, and it was about to start.

"Give it back immediately!" I yelled at her.

She kept laughing and hid behind Mom. "I want to watch Cartoon Network," she declared.

We started to wrestle with each other for the remote controller. Tired of our antics, Mom groaned at us. "Both of you, stop it!"

None of us listened to her. I tried to grab Sarah's

hair. Using this technique, I could easily defeat her, but she had become cleverer and would not let me grab her hair.

Mom swept Sarah into her lap and kissed her rosy cheeks. "Sweetie, it's story time, isn't it? Today, Mama will tell you a story about a cherry dress fairy."

"No, I want to watch cartoons," Sarah insisted.

"Aw, then that fairy will be sad," Mom coaxed Sarah.
Upon Mom's continuous urging, finally Sarah handed me the TV remote.

"Phew..." I exhaled with relief and flopped on the sofa. I promised myself that I would never leave the remote ever again for my silly sister.

Mom stopped on her way to the bedroom and raised a finger. "Shobi, only thirty minutes, hear me? You already played games for two hours on your tablet, and your screen time is over."

"But Mom, this TV show ends in one hour!" I threw a tantrum, but Mom just frowned at me. In a bad mood, I watched the show. She hated that I watched TV.

After half an hour, Mom appeared from her bedroom. She turned off the TV and didn't care that I squirmed and begged to watch for a few more minutes.

"Mom, please! It's almost finished." "No means No," she declared.

"She acts like a dictator sometimes", I thought as I stomped to my room.

"Shobi, have you forgotten? We decided to play Scrabble tonight," she called out. Angry, I ignored her. "Okay son, but at least brush your teeth properly before going to bed."

I shut the door of my room, brushed my teeth, and sat on a soft floor cushion. I never went to bed without brushing my teeth. With Mom's help, I had built up a small library of books where I could read without Sarah's interference. That little demon had a bad habit of poking her nose into everything I did.

I missed the time when I used to read books and play hide and seek with Mom, but everything changed as I grew older. Several times when I asked her to play any game, she made excuses, saying she was busy.

I made myself lost in my small library just to kill the time. I was waiting for Dad, but as the clock chimed eleven, all tired I laid on the cushion.

When I opened my eyes, I found myself snug in bed with a soft pillow underneath my head and a quilt over my body. I smiled. Mom must have put me onto bed.

Despite the window curtains, my room was still bright. I heard Sarah and Mom outside and tried to sleep, not wanting to get up. Mom came into the room and called, "Get up Shobi. It's quarter to eleven now."

"Mom, I want to sleep some more," I moaned.

"It's too late, son." Don't you want to have breakfast with us?" She asked as she quickly reset my books in the shelf. "Why don't you put your books back in the shelf after you're finished?" She shook her head in disappointment. "You never put things back in their right place." Her voice switched from sweet to stern in the blink of an eye.

I rolled over and closed my eyes, determined to ignore her and stay in bed. I had no intention of getting up early, especially on a weekend. But Mom was persistent. Every morning, she woke me up at the crack of dawn, even on Saturdays and Sundays. I was lucky if I got to sleep in till 10 am, let alone 11. And all because she insisted that we have every meal together as a family. I just didn't get it. What was the big deal about eating together, anyway?

With my eyes shut, I was daydreaming when I suddenly remembered my important meeting with Dad. I jumped out of bed, rushed to the bathroom, and within moments, I saw him at the dining table. He seemed busy talking to Sarah. I lovingly wrapped my arms around his neck.

"Good morning, Dad. How are you?"

"Good morning, son. I'm good," he replied in a deep voice.

"Dad, I want that latest amusement video game which we saw in the supermarket last month," I said breathlessly.

"You bought the newest video game for your birthday only a month ago," he pointed out, holding a piece of Paratha with omelette.

"That was my birthday gift, Dad," I reminded him and sat on the chair beside him. "This is for winning the debate competition."

He nodded with a smile and turned to Mom for approval, who was pouring tea from a kettle into cups laid on the kitchen counter. She set the cups on the tray, stepped toward the dining table, and looked up.

"Why do you need another video game when you already have one?"

My smile of anticipation vanished. 'Mom, you have no idea about these things,' I said, trying to reason with her. 'Once the latest program is launched, previous versions become outdated.'

"'Outdated!' she replied, waving her hand dismissively. 'It still works, doesn't it?'

"'Yeah, but it's like using a flip phone in a smartphone world!' I exclaimed. 'All my friends have the latest version, and I'll be left behind.'

"'Well, maybe they're just wasting their money on unnecessary upgrades," she said, her voice firm. "Do you think money grows on trees?"

"'No, but...!'" I started to protest, but she cut me off.

"'No buts, young man. We won't waste money on something just because it's shiny and new.'"

I sighed, knowing the conversation was over. But I couldn't help feeling frustrated that she just didn't get it.

Like my other favourite activities, she absolutely hated it too that I played video games, moreover I was not allowed to play warfare games because she was strongly against violence. Didn't she know that it was just a game? Obviously, I would not play these games to experience violence. Every time I asked to play one of those games, she would say, "Even if you ask when you are sixteen, I will still say no." This really bothered me. The way I saw it, I would not be playing warfare games until I was in college. Yikes!

And to add insult to injury, she thought I was an addict just because I played for two or three hours on weekdays! I mean, what's the harm in that?! But no, she'd always say, 'One hour is enough.' I'll never understand how to make her see that gaming was my passion!

I had noticed that Dad also failed sometimes to convince her to let me play. It was not that she 'always' stopped me, but the percentage of saying 'No' was very high.

Chapter 3
My Annoying Mom

My mom is really loving, but also really strict. It's hard to know what she'll be like from one minute to the next. But against her horrible temprament, she's very pretty and tall. Her skin is a beautiful honey color. Her big brown eyes are always shiny, even when she's upset. I can't help but notice her big brown eyes that always shine beneath perfectly shaped eyebrows even when she is angry. Her thin, pink lips just fit her perfectly. A scarf is always wrapped around her head, but when she gets mad, it is as if she turns into a stepparent from those Cinderella movies - not being able to help but find fault in everything her stepchildren does. This resembles the time when the Football World Cup had taken over everyone's attention.

Mom and Dad were like opposites when it came to watching sports with me. Dad loved staying up late to watch matches with me, but Mom hated it. It seemed like she didn't like anything I wanted to do! While Dad and I cheered on France and Brazil in the semi-finals, Mom was busy cooking in the kitchen. My sister Sarah was playing with her silly dolls, which looked even sillier after she drew tattoos on their faces with a blue pen. It was like we were all doing our own thing, but Mom and I were like oil and water - we just didn't mix!

"Hey Dad, look! That player's got a cool tattoo on his hand!" I exclaimed, pointing at the TV screen. Just then, Mom looked up from setting the table and said, "Son, tattoos are permanent and you shouldn't get them."

I was surprised and asked, "Why not?! I think they're awesome and I want one on my arm!"

Mom gave me one of her serious looks, and Dad chuckled and said, "Well, maybe we can talk about it later, kiddo!" But I knew Mom had already made up her mind, and I wasn't going to convince her anytime soon. To add fuel to my desire for a tattoo, she teasingly reminded me,"You can't even tolerate the pain of an injection needle. How would you handle dozens of needles stabbing into your skin?"

I turned to Dad. "Does it really hurt?" He nodded, not looking away from the TV. "Yes, and we are Muslims. We are not allowed tattoos."

I was disappointed, but when a pizza commercial came on TV and my tummy started growling, I blurted out, "I want pizza for dinner!"

Dad chuckled, tickled me, and whispered, "Me too, but we need to convince Mom." So, I stood up on the couch, faced the kitchen, and yelled, "Mom, we're ordering pizza!"

She appeared in the doorway, holding a spatula with some rice sticking on it, and gave us a stern look. "Dinner will be served in a moment, and it will be delicious Biryani," As she turned, she added, "Wash your hands and hurry up before it gets cold."

I turned helplessly towards Dad, hoping for some backup, but he simply shrugged, smiled, and motioned me toward the table.

'Yes, honey,' he said, like he always did. In moments, he was sitting happily at the dinner table, the pizza forgotten.

I sometimes got confused about how a person could change their mind so fast. A minute ago, he was

excited to eat pizza with me, and the next minute, he was okay with a homemade meal. It had always surprised me that all adults wanted to have their meals at home. What could I say about Mom, how could she say 'No' to her family when they craved pizza?

It never made any sense to me. Why did Mom always insist on serving pulses with rice or fish curry and bread? It wasn't fair! I could never understand what was so fascinating about that? How could it possibly compare to a juicy, cheesy burger? Dad always gave in to her, trying to keep his wife happy by appreciating her cooking, and at those moments, my heart always cried out, 'Oh, come on, Dad! Let's not underestimate the deliciousness of an OPTP sizzling burger!' And, of course, Dad would exaggerate things, because that's what dads do, right?

A few days later, Sarah and I decided to play with our toys. Despite our quarrels and differences, we would sometimes play like loving siblings. This usually only happened when she listened to me; otherwise, our games often ended in her screaming. At my suggestion, she brought out all of her stuffed toys and I built an enormous house with toy building blocks.

"Let's park my cars outside and make a small farmhouse for the toy animals," I suggested, and she happily agreed. After two hours of tiring effort, we finished our project.

"Mom, come and see what we made!" Sara exclaimed

as she went to get her from the balcony where Mom was pinning laundry to dry.

"Whoa, this is amazing!" Mom exclaimed, her eyes wide with surprise. "You two have worked so hard on this project! I can't believe how creative you are!" She beamed with pride. "But remember, in 30 minutes, you need to clean up and put everything back in its place, okay?" She reminded us with a gentle smile. "I'm feeling a bit tired, sweetie," she said to me, "so can you please keep an eye on your sister for a bit while I take a quick nap?"

I nodded and continued my play with Sarah. Our creative minds wanted more exercise, so we decided to expand our project. After half an hour, our toy farmhouse looked great with decorative toys. We pretended to be residents of this beautiful setting. We even used some kitchen utensils and colourful flower arrangements, which Mom bought from a nearby flower shop last weekend, including pillows and cushions to make a castle beside our toy house. We were happy with what we had created.

After sometime, Mom appeared from her room and her jaw dropped. "Oh, my God, Shoaib! Sarah! What a mess you both have created. I told you to put your toys away after half an hour." Her voice warned us that something was wrong. Sarah and I looked at each other.

"But Mom, we were just playing," Sarah replied innocently. Mom kept staring at us, both hands on her waist.

"Shobi, put every single one of your countless toys back into the chest in your room. And Sarah, get those stuffed dolls out of my sight and store them properly in your cupboard! I can't take this clutter anymore!" Mom's tone was harsh and her frustration with our messiness was evident.

Annoyed, I raised my hands in frustration. 'Mom, I'm tired!' I complained, but her stern look silenced me, warning me not to say another word. I knew better than to argue, so I reluctantly did as I was told.

From that day, I had some strong opinions about my mom. She was a cleanliness freak. Secondly, she was mean like my school headmistress. Furthermore, she wanted everyone, including my five-year-old sister, to be well-mannered at the table, in the bedroom, in the park, in the living room, and at family gatherings. Oh yeah, and in the bathroom too… It was infuriating how controlling and rigid she can be sometimes.

Chapter 4
The Outings

The past weekend was an amazing adventure as we visited the Pakistan Air Force Museum. It was a vast and captivating space, brimming with history and stunning displays that left us in awe. It had indoor and outdoor exhibits of vintage aeroplanes, fighters, helicopters, and amusement rides, surrounded by an enormous garden fit for a royal palace. First, we entered a lush green park with colourful flowers and decorations. A refreshing cool breeze welcomed us there as we strolled on the red-stoned path. Beautiful flowers lined the path, their fragrance filling the air. Some people sat with their families on the grass. Children's shouts and birds chirping added life to the pleasant atmosphere. Smoky clouds partially covered a brilliant blue sky, the whole sight was pleasing to the soul.

Mom held my hand as we strolled along the path, leading toward the central building where war scenes were on display. But I suddenly broke free from her grip and ran off, eager to explore the exhibits on my own.

Dad called out after me, "Shoaib, wait for us!" But I wanted to explore, arms spread like a plane, weaving among the people, turning to smoothly balance my body. I stopped in front of a giant aeroplane that struck me with awe and made me stand still. I was like a small insect before that giant.

'C-130, a troop and cargo transport aircraft with four engines,' I read aloud from the nearby display board. But before I could continue, Mom grasped my arm and gave me a gentle shake. "Shobi, what's gotten into you? Can't you see it's crowded here and you could get lost?' she asked, her voice filled with concern.

As I hung my head in shame and dragged myself toward Dad, who was standing next to Sarah, he admonished me. "Shoaib, don't ever wander off like that again!"

I felt rebellious, though. Mom always kept me by her side when we went out, which really annoyed me. Despite feeling grown up and capable of taking care of myself, she treated me like a toddler. Perhaps she feared for herself, getting lost because her sense of direction wasn't the best.

After a few fulfilling hours of enjoyment, we made our way back home feeling fatigued from all the fun.

The days passed fairly quickly, and before I knew it, the holy month of Ramadan had arrived. Ramadan had always fascinated me, as it brought a sense of excitement and community. We were accustomed to going to the mosque at night more than at any other time.

One night, as everyone was getting ready to leave for the mosque, I searched frantically for my white prayer cap. 'Mom, where's my Namaz Cap?' I asked, exasperated.

She replied calmly, "Look in the drawer, sweetie."

But after rummaging through it, I couldn't find it. Mom then reached in and effortlessly pulled out the cap, which had been right in front of me. As she handed it to me and hurried off, I couldn't help but kick myself for not spotting it earlier.

"She has eagle eyes," I thought to myself, a smile spreading across my face.

Once we were all settled in and Dad started the car, we hit the road, which was packed with traffic. The minaret speakers echoed loud prayer calls, creating an enchanting atmosphere. Everyone was eager to reach the mosque on time for the special Ramadan prayers, and I always loved this energetic and lively hustle and bustle.

We walked into the crowded mosque and separated towards the men's and women's sections. Like the exterior, the interior decorations were modestly done with white walls and colored carpets that created a feeling of Allah being with us. Some people immersed

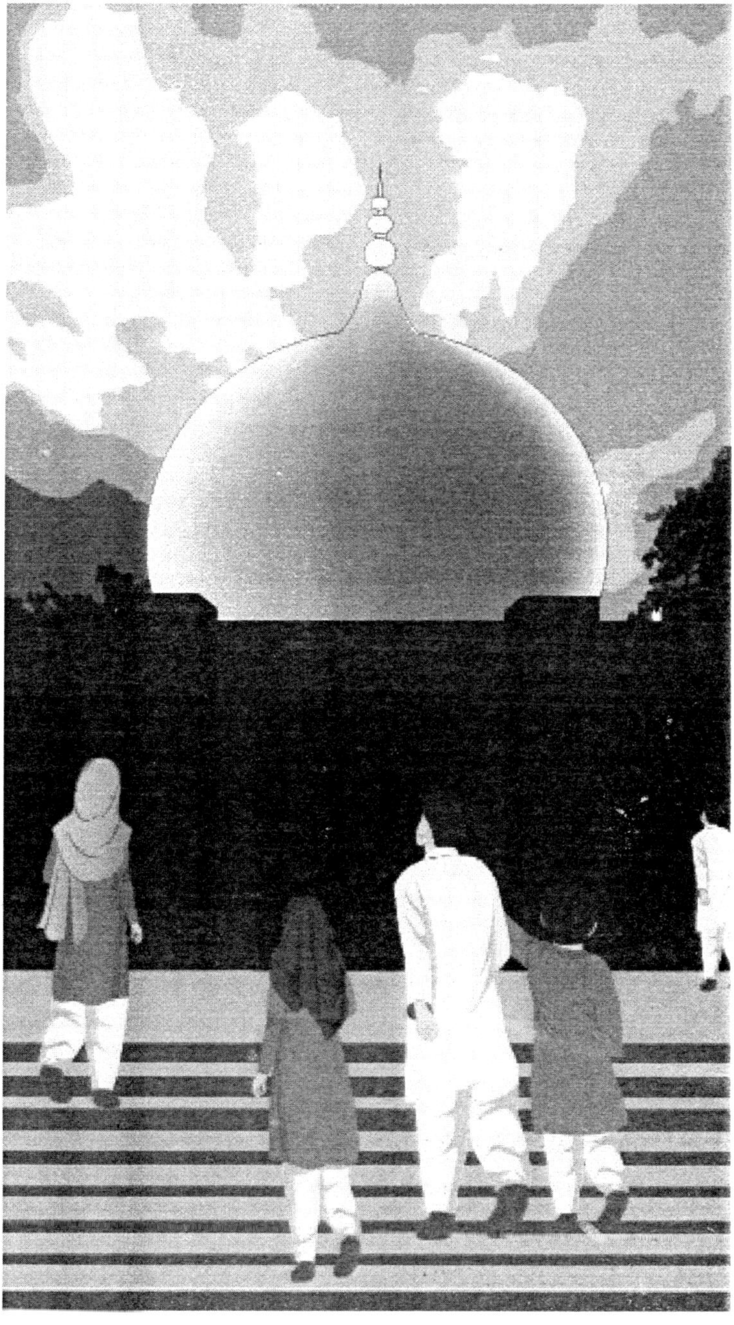

themselves in whispered religious conversations as we waited for the Imam to lead us in prayer. I prayed with Dad for a while and then went to play with other boys behind the worshipers. A man in uniform kept an eye on all of us to prevent any brawls. I remembered Mom's daily reminder before we left the mosque. "Shobi, we never disturb the worshippers, so be careful not to make any noise."

There was no need to say that all the time though...

On the way back, Sarah dozed off in the car. I turned to Dad and said, "I want to fast with you tomorrow."

He replied, 'You can try, but it's better if you wait until next year when you'll be eleven years old."

Mom chimed in, "Your father is right, honey."

Although I was disappointed with their decision, I remained silent.

Ramadan was nice, but I was more excited when it was about to end because we were able to go shopping for Eid. Mom loved shopping, and so did I. Dad took us to a new mall and Sarah and I immediately went through the colourful complex and found interesting activities.

"I wanna go to the fun area," Sarah insisted.

"I'm going to video arcade," I pulled Dad and he was about to let me, but as usual, Mom refused. "Let's do the shopping first, otherwise both of them will get tired and will pester us."

Downcast and with heavy feet, I followed them towards the shops. In a clothing store, a blue denim jacket looked amazing. I immediately pointed at it, but Mom shook her head. "No, Shobi. We are here to shop Kurta for Eid. Let's move to another section."

I sighed with frustration and longing for the jacket. While shopping last month for my aunt's wedding, I remembered how much I had liked a blue T-shirt with a Superman logo. However, Mom refused to buy it for me because she thought it was not suitable for the event. Though she did purchase another one that I also like, I still miss the blue one.

On the first weekend of every month, we used to go grocery shopping. This month, Dad took us to a new supermarket, which doubled my excitement. I always loved to go to a supermarket for groceries. As we drove into the underground multi-story parking area of the huge superstore, it seemed like the whole city was there to shop as well. This meant that we couldn't find a parking space.

After fifteen minutes of searching, Dad finally succeeded in finding a parking spot when another car left. He quickly parked as another driver had their eye on the same spot. We all breathed a sigh of relief, except for Sarah. She never seemed to worry about these kinds of problems.

As we walked toward the sleek automatic glass door, it smoothly slid open. Following the crowd, we entered the self-service shops offering a wide variety of foods and household products. The complex was larger than our usual grocery store, but customers still pushed and shoved each other as they tried to gain access to the many bargains. Mom extracted a grocery list from her purse.

I raised my hand eagerly and said, "Give me the list, Mom! I'll get everything for you."

"It's my turn to do the shopping, Mom, Brother did it last time, so now it's my turn." As usual, Sarah contradicted me, trying to take the responsibility for herself.

"Shoaib, please go and get a trolley," Dad requested. I quickly dashed off to fetch one, and we began making our way through the lanes, carefully selecting our desired items. The store was bustling with people expertly navigating their trolleys to make way for each other.

Suddenly, a boy around Sarah's age let out a loud whine and tried to wriggle free from his mother's grasp as they passed us by. His white and blue trainers screeched against the polished marble floor as he struggled to break free. Finally, he managed to slip away and sprinted off towards the toy section. I could see Sarah looking at him with longing in her eyes, also wanting to go there.

Mom said, "After we get everything on our list, we can visit the kids' section." But first, she asked, "Who can get me the butter?" She held my hand tight so I wouldn't run off.

Sarah quickly ran to the dairy section and brought back the butter. Then, Mom let me weigh the fruits and veggies - I loved trying to guess how much they weighed as I put them on the scale.

After gathering all the items, we went to the kids' section. Despite the crowd, Sarah and I managed to make our way through it. Sarah immediately picked up a small stuffed silky brown teddy bear, while I chose a large box containing a remote-controlled Lamborghini.

Mom and Dad exchanged glances, and she shook her head saying, "Sweetie, choose a smaller one. This one is too big to play with in your room."

"No, Mom. I love this car. I will manage."

"Shobi, it's very expensive. Pick another."

After further urging and not very happy, I agreed to take two small dinky cars and we returned home.

"Every time, it's Sarah who gets what she wants," I complained bitterly, sitting straight with arms folded across my chest, promising myself that this time, I would not leave her stupid teddy alone. As usual, Mom ignored my complaint.

For a few days afterwards, I failed to find an opportunity to take my revenge as Sarah hardly left the teddy bear for a second. It had become her favorite toy, but after a couple of weeks when Mom was showering her, I snuck into her bedroom and searched for it. While hearing chattering from mother-daughter in the bathroom, I found it on her bed under a pillow with its shiny black buttoned eyes staring at me. Filled with hate, I held onto it tightly and pulled its arm until white cotton peeked out. Satisfied, I threw it back onto the bed and ran away. A sense of satisfaction washed over me as I looked back to see Sarah crying for their beloved toy.

Lately, Mom's constant nagging was becoming very annoying.

"Why is this wet towel still lying on the bed?"
"Brush your teeth."
"Clean your room."
"Have you offered prayers?"
"Put your toys back in the chest."
"Why haven't you finished your lunch yet?"
"Don't tease your sister."
"Turn off the TV now, your screen time is over."
Blah blah...

I was really annoyed when Mom gushed over me at the parent-teacher meeting. She said stuff like, "My son is a genius! He's super smart, hardworking, he rides his bike so carefully, he is very sensible..."

It was embarrassing. I wondered why she praised me so much in public but nagged me all the time at home. It seemed like she knew everything about me, even the fights I got into or the extra chocolate I sneaked. It was like she had a magic mirror that showed her everything I did.

I felt like she was always watching me, always waiting for me to make a mistake so she could address it with me. It was like I couldn't even breathe without her knowing about it. And the worst part was, she always had to be right. She never listened to my side of the story or tried to understand what I was going through. She just assumed she knew everything and that I was always wrong.

It was so frustrating! I felt like I was walking on eggshells all the time, never knowing when she would have a concern about something I did. And the praise at the parent-teacher meeting just made it worse. It was like she was trying to show off or something. I just wished she would understand me better and treat me like a normal kid for once. But no, she had to keep guiding me with her constant feedback and praise. It was like she was trying to help me too much

Chapter 5
Consistent Problems

It seemed that my Mom and I had a series of ongoing disputes that would never end, like the one we had on Saturday evening after Ramadan. Unlike other weekends, we were at home due to hot weather outside caused by a heatwave in Karachi. April typically wasn't too hot, but that year was an exception. The only option was to stay home in the evening and play with my Legos.

After Mom set the table for supper, she called us to come eat. Dad appeared from his room, busy tapping on his mobile phone. Bored of playing with Legos, I turned on the TV just as Mom called my name. "Shobi, come to the table," she said, "we are waiting for you."

Mom settled Sarah next to her and served all of us. I heard the jingle of my favorite cartoon show on TV, so I quickly filled my plate with kebabs, pickled cucumbers from a mixed salad, and rushed towards the sofa in front of the TV. I was excited to watch Ben Ten while eating dinner when she called out, "Supper is a family gathering, and no one leaves the table until it's over."

"But Mom, my favorite show is on. I don't want to miss theis episode," I wailed in despair.

But as usual, Mom remained unmoved. "Shobi, you watched that same episode yesterday. Come join us at the table so we can eat together."

"What's wrong with watching TV while eating?" I was only interested in the TV show, not eating with the family. I didn't mean any harm, but Dad was stunned at my reaction and Mom even more. I could feel the anger boiling inside her, but I was upset that I could not have my meal where I wanted to, so I marched out of the lounge, slamming the door behind me. Mom kept calling me, but I didn't listen.

After some time, I reflected on what I had done that day. I not only missed my favourite TV show, but I also managed to make Mom and Dad angry with me. I guess it was wrong of me to dislike her for trying to discipline me, but I sometimes found it hard not to. Later, I managed to sort it out with her, but what was done was done.

A few days later, another problem arose. My Urdu teacher accused me of disturbing the class and gave me a complaint letter about my behavior. At first, I thought to tear it up and throw it away, but I was well aware of the consequences in case my parents didn't address this type of situation. There was no other option but to face Mom directly and endure any punishment that may come with it, so I did not choose that route.

When I got home, I rushed to my room leaving Mom amazed. As I sat on my bed, troubled and scratching my head trying to think of how to deal with this new hurdle, it was clear that having a fine brain like mine meant no shortage of ideas. And just as quickly as the thought came, a brilliant idea hit me. With precision, I placed the letter in the side pocket of my bag where the water bottle was kept and opened its cap ever so slightly that any small jolt would cause the water to leak out onto it. Feeling confident with my plan in place, I put on my backpack and started jumping around the room. After making sure that every inch of the letter was completely wet, I left my bag on the floor and went for a shower feeling proud of myself for coming up with such an ingenious solution. It was a well set accident.

"Come for lunch, honey." Mom knocked at my room's door. I hugged her warmly and followed her like an obedient son.

"Is everything all right, Shobi?" She demanded, looking closely at me.

"Oh yes, Mom, all is good," I exclaimed. Before sitting down, I pulled Sarah's ponytail and she squealed in protest.

"Behave yourself, Shobi, and don't pull her hair again!" Mom scolded.

As soon as I began eating, I suddenly remembered something important. "Oh Mom, I forgot to tell you - my Urdu teacher has a letter for you." I pretended as there was no important business otherthan having my meal.

"Bring it to me," Mom said.

I sighed and replied, "Mom, I've asked you several times to buy me a new water bottle because mine is leaking." But she wasn't going to be distracted from the matter at hand. She firmly said, "Bring me your bag."

Reluctantly, I went back to my room and grabbed

discipline me, but I sometimes found it hard not to. Later, I managed to sort it out with her, but what was done was done.

A few days later, another problem arose. My Urdu teacher accused me of disturbing the class and gave me a complaint letter about my behavior. At first, I thought to tear it up and throw it away, but I was well aware of the consequences in case my parents didn't address this type of situation. There was no other option but to face Mom directly and endure any punishment that may come with it, so I did not choose that route.

When I got home, I rushed to my room leaving Mom amazed. As I sat on my bed, troubled and scratching my head trying to think of how to deal with this new hurdle, it was clear that having a fine brain like mine meant no shortage of ideas. And just as quickly as the thought came, a brilliant idea hit me. With precision, I placed the letter in the side pocket of my bag where the water bottle was kept and opened its cap ever so slightly that any small jolt would cause the water to leak out onto it. Feeling confident with my plan in place, I put on my backpack and started jumping around the room. After making sure that every inch of the letter was completely wet, I left my bag on the floor and went for a shower feeling proud of myself for coming up with such an ingenious solution. It was a well set accident.

"Come for lunch, honey." Mom knocked at my room's door. I hugged her warmly and followed her like an obedient son.

"Is everything all right, Shobi?" She demanded, looking closely at me.

"Oh yes, Mom, all is good," I exclaimed. Before sitting down, I pulled Sarah's ponytail and she squealed in protest.

"Behave yourself, Shobi, and don't pull her hair again!" Mom scolded.

As soon as I began eating, I suddenly remembered something important. "Oh Mom, I forgot to tell you - my Urdu teacher has a letter for you." I pretended as there was no important business otherthan having my meal.

"Bring it to me," Mom said.

I sighed and replied, "Mom, I've asked you several times to buy me a new water bottle because mine is leaking." But she wasn't going to be distracted from the matter at hand. She firmly said, "Bring me your bag."

Reluctantly, I went back to my room and grabbed

the bag. As expected, when we found the letter inside it was all wet - exactly as planned.

"See what the leaking bottle has done to the letter?" I told her. "Please write a note to the teacher about this and she will give me another one on Monday."

My brain was functioning smarter than before. I considered the possibility of approaching Miss Faheema during this one day grace period with good behavior and a sincere apology, confident that she would accept it without my mother ever finding out about the incident. It seemed as though everything was turning in my favor.

Silently, Mom got up and headed to the iron stand. My heart sank when I realized what she was about to do. "It's not fair," I thought miserably. I was boiling inside with anger seeing my clever plan ruined by an iron.

As Mom read the complaint letter, her face seemed to stiffen and turned red. I braced myself for a stern lecture, knowing my smart brain would be of no use this time. It wasn't entirely my fault - all I did was have a little fun with my friend Abdul Rehman during a boring lecture. We weren't supposed to talk in class, so I threw a paper plane at him with a secret message.

However, Miss Faheema happened to be writing on the whiteboard when it swooped out of control and landed at her feet.

She turned and glared at the entire class before demanding, "Who did this?"

Nobody said a thing. Miss Faheema put down her board marker, removed her rimless spectacles, and again demanded an answer. This time several students pointed at me. She scolded me brutally in front of the whole class. I tried to justify myself, but she didn't listen. That's when she wrote the letter.

"Shobi, what is this?" Mom asked harshly. "Why did you throw a paper plane during class?"

"I was simply asking my friend about his new remote-controlled car," I mumbled.

"Was that really so important that it disrupted the whole class?" she scolded me.

"But Mom, what's wrong with asking?" I couldn't understand her reaction.

"Your teacher has every right to suspend you for three days because of your disruptive behavior in class. Your actions have consequences and can affect others in a negative way. Tomorrow, we will talk to Miss Faheema. But from now on, no more complaints like this."

"You are just like my horrible teacher. She hardly ever spoke nicely to me," I shouted.

Mom froze in shock as I jumped up and marched out, slamming the door behind me. It had become normal practice for me and my Mom to argue. She just doesn't understand me.

Chapter 6
A Fight

In the evening, I got ready for some fresh air.

"Mom! I'm going cycling with my friends," I announced and left. I wasn't in the mood to hear her safety instructions. "It's better to avoid her," I assured myself. Hanging around her always led to an argument and ended with lectures, so a smart person like me preferred keeping distance from such situations.

Outside, I saw Umar talking to his mother, Aunty Salma. I couldn't help but think that he was so lucky to have a mom like Aunty Salma who always showered him with love and never scolded or yelled at him.

Aunty Salma handed him the helmet, smiled, and

waved goodbye. As we moved off, our friends joined us.

"Let's go to the main road," Usman suggested.

"No, my mama doesn't allow me to ride on the main road," Umar protested.

"Let's just head to the main park then," I said, even though Mom had previously forbidden me from going there due to some rowdy teenagers who bothered us before. Everyone agreed and we set off. The weather was pleasant and we pedaled hard to outdo each other.

In our group, Hasan was the naughtiest. He used to poke his nose into matters that did not concern him. He was a skinny but tall boy with sharp features and small eyes. We all agreed that it was his extraordinary nose that pushed him to get involved in everything.

As we approached the park, we saw the teenagers playing cricket. We could hear their shouts celebrating boundaries and wickets. Hasan became more focused on their game than cycling. Suddenly, one boy hit the ball so hard that it came straight toward us and hit Usman on his head. He staggered and tumbled to the ground with his cycle. He sat up and groaned in pain. We crowded around him.

"Oh no! You've got bruises on your elbow and knee," Hasan said, concern filling his voice. "Thank goodness you wore a helmet, or it could have been much worse!" He shook his head, relieved. "Those bullies need to learn a lesson!"

Hasan picked up the ball and tossed it over the fence, and we all burst out laughing. But our giggles were short-lived, as two angry teens marched towards us. We weren't afraid, but we knew it wouldn't be smart to fight them.

The teens approached us, their faces red with anger. "How dare you throw my ball away?" One of them groaned.

We were scared, but we didn't run away. Without a second thought, Hasan fearlessly stood up to confront the young boy. "You should have been more responsible! That ball could have caused some serious harm," he said firmly.

In response, the older kid forcefully pushed Hasan across his shoulder and menacingly challenged: "What are you gonna do about it?"

I stepped forward, my voice steady. "Leave him alone!"

He suddenly turned towards me and violently gripped my shoulder, causing excruciating pain that coursed through every part of my body. Then he grabbed my collar with both hands and lifted me off the ground. I was scared but realized it was time to teach that bully a lesson. Curling my fingers into a fist, I punched his nose with all my force.

Blood poured out and he staggered back, clutching his nose. Taking advantage of this opportunity, I pushed him hard and he lost his balance, falling to the ground and groaning in pain. His friends rushed over to help him sit up while mine looked on in shock.

"Oh my God! He is bleeding," one of the boys shouted and turned toward me. "See what have you done, you idiot!"

I stepped back in fear. As the sounds around me faded, my heart beat faster and my legs struggled to support my weight. I quickly grabbed my bicycle and raced off, determined to get home as soon as possible so I could hide away and forget what had just happened.

"Fighting is not the solution to any problem, sweetheart," Mom's voice echoed in my ears, but it was too late. Wishing to be a hero among my friends, I was in big trouble.

Ashen-faced and shaking like a leaf, I pedaled my bike home, my heart racing with dread. When I walked in the door, Mom's eyes widened in alarm.

"Shobi, what's wrong? You look like you've seen a ghost!"

But I couldn't muster a word, my voice trapped in

my throat. I fled to my room, collapsing onto the bed as if my legs had given out. I clasped my head in my hands, desperate to think of a way out of this mess, but for once, my wit had abandoned me. Just as Mom knocked at my door, the doorbell rang, making my heart skip a beat.

"Oh no, what if... what if the boy was seriously hurt? What if the police were here to take me away?" I slowly walked out of my room, and to my vast relief, saw Umar and Hasan's familiar faces.

"What happened? Why are you here?" I asked anxiously. "Is the boy all right?"

They both looked at each other and burst out laughing. "You big coward! When you raced off, my daddy came. He saw everything," Umar told me.

"Really?" My heart sank because I knew that now, Umar's mother would tell my mom all about my not-so-heroic act.

"He did. He scolded those boys for their misbehaviour and sent them to a nearby dispensary," Hasan replied. "That guy is fine now."

"'And then he warned them to stick to the playground,' Umar added, his eyes wide with excitement, as if he was recalling the drama all over again."

As I exhaled a sigh of relief, a weight lifted off my chest. In that moment, I made a silent promise to myself: no more fighting.

For the first time, I agreed with Mom that fighting was not a solution to any problem.

As I bid farewell to my friends and turned to leave, Mom's firm grip on my arm steered me toward the sofa. Her stern expression was a clear warning: no more trouble.

"I just got a call from Aunty Salma," she began, her voice firm but concerned. "She told me about the fight. Is it true?" Her stern expression warned me not to cause more trouble for myself.

I didn't have enough courage to look her in the eyes.

"They started the fight. One of them grabbed my collar, and in self-defense, I hit him." Words hardly came out of my mouth.

She stared at me for several long seconds. "You are grounded for a week."

"What!? But why? I didn't do anything wrong," I protested, but she didn't listen. I literally hated her at that moment.

Apart from going to school, I spent the the whole week at home. I had no choice but to listen to her constant criticism, which made my home a prison, and she was the warden.

Chapter 7
An Accident

The days passed by uneventfully, and my studies kept me very busy. School assignments and tests, everything pressed on me so much that I lost my appetite. At school, the atmosphere was full of stress, and at home, Mom kept nagging me. At last, the final exams arrived. Worried and nervous, constantly tired of Mom's never-ending reminders to study hard, served to make me dispirited. I couldn't take it any longer, and one day, I exploded, "Mom, please! Can't you just leave me alone?"

The look of shock on her face made it clear that she wasn't expecting such harsh words from me. As soon as she left the room without saying a word, I regretted my outburst and scolded myself for being so rude. However, in that moment when all I wanted was to be left alone, after seeing her walk away, I thanked God that she left me alone for a while. This happiness lasted only a day. The next morning, Mom showed up with new study plans. Reluctantly, I couldn't help but admire her determination and cleverness in finding ways to motivate me towards success...

My efforts and her diligence were rewarded, and I passed my final exams with flying colours. Mom and Dad were very happy and congratulated me, but that changed nothing between two of us. Our antagonism continued, as did our arguments. We barely ever came to an agreement on anything. It's like we're from different planets or something.

The following day, we were all gathered in the lounge with a cheerful energy. After acing my exams, I knew it was time for a reward and as always, Dad let me choose what to get.

"Dad," I said casually, "I'm thinking of getting a hoverboard this time."

Mom looked at me skeptically and asked, "Isn't that meant for teenagers?"

"Absolutely not, Mom." I resisted strongly. Mom kept staring at me. "And what if it is? I'm ten years old now," I reminded her.

Mom did not look convinced, but I buttered her a lot until she agreed. Next weekend, Dad bought me the newest model of the exact hoverboard I wanted. Although he too was not entirely in favour of getting it, I didn't let anyone spoil my happiness this time.

When I first tried riding the hoverboard, I took a tumble - but I refused to let that stop me! I learned that perseverance is key to mastering the hoverboard.

With determination and practice, I finally found my balance by simply shifting my weight. Dad was a great coach, helping me practice on weekends, and soon I was riding like a pro every day. It just goes to show that with persistence and patience, you can conquer any challenge that comes your way.

I chuckled at my mother's constant worrying and reminders to always be safe. "Shobi, take it easy and don't ride so fast," she would say every time I hopped on my hoverboard. But in reality, her precautions made me feel like I was heading into a treacherous battlefield rather than simply going for a ride.

After gaining experience using it, my longtime dream of adventure was finally fulfilled. Moments like these made all my hard work and dedication worth every second. I proudly showed it off to my friends.

"Wow, that's cool." Everyone was impressed, which made me even happier.

One evening as I rode the board, showing my friends the latest stunt I had learnt, few boys from another street came towards me. I instantly recognized one of them as the same guy that I had punched in the nose before. It was like a déjà vu moment for me. He wore blue jeans with ripped knees and a white T-shirt. His two friends were almost dressed alike. They were chewing gum and their continuous stares made me uncomfortable. This time they all were riding hoverboards.

I tried to ignore them and kept myself busy with my friends, but the boys seemed to have some bad intentions. They started to encircle us on their hoverboards. None of us wanted to mess with them again, but the boy I punched pointed at me and mocked, "Hey, you bloke! Do you have the guts to do some stunts, huh? Come race with me."

"I'm not interested," I told him.

They laughed, "Hey kid, are you afraid?"

My blood boiled. "I'm not afraid of anyone." I tried to act calmly, but their laughter drove me crazy and I zoomed past them.

My friends called after me, "Shoaib, stop! Don't listen to them!" but I ignored their cries.

The boys laughed continuously as they chased after me. I increased my speed, tilting my body slightly, and pushed my right foot forward while keeping the other horizontal, allowing me to make a smooth turn. Their laughter turned to cheers as they struggled to keep up with me. Determined to outdo them, I showcased my exceptional hoverboard skills, executing a spin that left them in awe. Not everyone could pull off such a move, and I knew it. With a confident push of my feet in opposite directions, I spun around, leaving the boys in my dust..

What a sight that was! In surprise they all stood still. Evidently, they were not expecting me doing such stunt.

With a boost of confidence, I rode my hoverboard really fast, wanting to show them how good I was.

As soon as I turned the corner, I saw a car zooming straight at me! I tried to move out of the way, but it was too late. The car hit me hard, and I flew up into the air. I landed on the hard road with a painful thud. It was like a giant hand came down and slammed a door shut on me! My right side felt numb, and I couldn't move a muscle. I was frozen like a statue.

Two men sprinted and leaned over me, their hands grasping my cheeks, and gently slapped them to rouse me from my daze.

Everything seemed to happen in slow motion like a dream. I heard their muffled voices, but the words were indistinguishable. As I slowly regained consciousness, I became aware of my battered body, and a wave of pain washed over me. I burst into uncontrollable sobs. I heard them say something, but I couldn't understand them. At last, I could feel my aching body and I started to cry nonstop.

By then, a whole lot of people had gathered around me, looking worried.

Chapter 8
An Angel

Someone must have told Mom about my accident. I saw her pull up in the car. She jumped out and ran towards me, looking worried. The people around me helped her get me into the car. As we drove to the hospital, she kept trying to calm down me.

"Just a few more minutes, sweetie. We're almost there. Don't worry, dear. Everything will be fine."

My forehead bled, and my head throbbed like a drum. When we got to the hospital, two men in white uniforms came running out to help me like superheroes. They gently lifted me onto a gurney, but even that slightest move made me cry out "Ow!" I looked around frantically for Mom. She was right behind me, like a guardian angel. She was talking to the doctors, trying to figure out what was wrong with me. But then, a nurse came over and started examining me. Once again, severe pain made me squirm. But then, Mom held my hand, and it was like she had superpowers. She made me feel a little better, and I found the courage to face the agony. Despite all our differences, at that moment, I only wanted her with me.

"Hey Shobi, don't worry, okay? You're going to be just fine, my brave superhero son!" Mom whispered to me, trying to make me feel better. And it worked!.

The nurse had given me some special medicine to help with the pain, and I finally stopped sobbing. She also put a special bandage on my forehead. Later, they took me to a special room called radiology to take a picture of my arm with a big X-ray machine. It was like a secret spy tool.

"The doctor told me, "You've got a broken arm, but don't worry! We'll fix it up with a plaster cast. It'll be good as new in six weeks. And the good news is, your other injuries are minor, and you'll be back to normal in no time, God willing."

Just then, Dad arrived at the hospital from work, and after a little while, he drove Mom and me home, safe and sound.

As we drove home, I suddenly realized Sarah was

missing.

"Where's Sarah?" I asked, feeling a bit worried.

Mom gave me a gentle smile and said, "Don't worry, sweetie, she's with Aunty Salma. She's in good hands!"

As soon as we got home, Dad helped me snuggle into bed, and I felt a wave of relief wash over me. "Shobi, you're looking a bit better!" he said, trying to sound cheerful. "Tell me all about what happened—"

But Mom jumped in, her eyes filled with concern. "Not now, dear. Let's get you both some food first. I'm sure you're both famished!" She smiled softly and hurried out of the room, leaving me feeling grateful and loved. Just then, I realized that Mom somehow knew exactly what I was thinking - that I wasn't ready to talk about the scary accident yet. It was like she had a special superpower that let her understand me without me even saying a word!

I was lying on my bed with my eyes half closed and my plastered arm across my chest, supported by a sling around my neck. My bandaged head was still spinning. I tried to forget whatever happened few hours ago, but my brain was like a movie screen, replaying the scary moments over and over... Sarah came into the room and gazed at me with a combination of sadness and love on her face. I felt the warmth of her love and worry for me. She came slowly to the bed but didn't say a word. Dad hugged her. "Your brother is fine, sweetheart. He's just hurt a little."

She nodded silently, and two small tears rolled down her rosy cheeks, which she immediately wiped with her small palms. I discovered something very precious that day. I had never realized that my sister loved me. To me, she was just a pesky sibling- a rabble router, but I was absolutely wrong.

Mom walked in with a big smile, carrying a steaming bowl of my favorite soup and some crispy chicken nuggets that made my tummy happy. She sat down beside me, gave me a gentle hug, and said, "Hey, son, time to fuel up and feel better! Don't worry about what happened, we'll talk about it later, okay?" She looked over at Dad, and he nodded in agreement, like he always did when Mom had a great idea.

The next morning, as I slowly opened my eyes, I found Mom beside me, her exhausted eyes shining with love and concern. She had stayed up all night, watching over me like a guardian angel, making sure I was safe and sound. As soon as I moved, she sprang into action, giving me a gentle kiss on the forehead. "How's my brave boy doing today?" she asked, her voice trembling with emotion, as she softly stroked my hair with her tired fingers. I could see the weight of worry on her face, but she was still smiling for me, trying to hide her fears.

I tried to sit up, but my body felt like it was made of lead, and every movement hurt. Mom quickly came to my rescue, helping me out of bed and supporting me as I took a few wobbly steps to the bathroom. It felt like a marathon, but with Mom by my side, I knew I could make it.

I remembered how she had held Sarah's hands when she took her first steps, never letting her fall. "She must have held me like that when I was little," I thought. I had never seen my Mom so worried, and Sarah that quiet. It took a little time to come to terms with my horrible accident and to understand that whatever Mom said was for my safety. Tears pricked my eyes. It wasn't because of my aching body, but my aching heart. I felt a lump form in my throat as I realized how much my family loved me, and how much they had been hurting alongside me.

As Mom brought in my breakfast, Sarah followed her, beaming with her brightest Cheshire smile. It lit up the whole room, and filled my heart with love. I realised how much I missed her smile. Without it, I was unable to recognise her.

Mom set the tray down and gave me a gentle kiss on the forehead. "How are you feeling today, sweetie?"

"I'm feeling a little better, Mom," I replied, trying to sound brave.

Sarah crept closer, her messy noodle hair bouncing with each step. "I have a surprise for you, brother!" she announced, her voice barely containing her excitement.

"What is it, Sarah?" I asked, curiously.

With her eyes shining like diamonds, she revealed her beloved brown teddy bear, its paw wrapped in a tiny bandage. "I wanted to share Mr. Whiskers with you, because he makes me feel better when I'm sad or hurt," she explained..

I felt a lump in my throat as I looked at Sarah's sweet face. She was trying so hard to make me feel better, and it was working! I smiled, and she smiled back, and for a moment, everything felt okay again.

"Thank you, Sarah! That's so sweet of you!"

Mom smiled, her eyes welling up with tears. "That's my little girl, always spreading love and joy."

In that moment, I felt the warmth of family's love flood back into my heart, like a cozy hug that chased away all the hurt and fear. That moment was the moment of realization.

My Mom's love is like a cooling treat,
On a hot summer day, it can't be beat.
She worries about me, and shows she cares,
Like a gentle breeze that's always there.

Her voice is soft, like leaves in the trees,
Guiding me along, with gentle ease.
Her love is like rain, that helps me sleep,
And fills my heart, with a happy deep.

She's like a rainbow, with colors so bright,
Loving, caring, and sometimes a little tight!
But I know she's always looking out for me,
My guardian angel, a love that's just right!

At night, when Mom wished me sweet dreams, I held her hand and told her all about the accident, apologizing deeply. "I'm sorry, Mom," I sobbed, and a tear rolled out. "I'm sorry that I thought you were wrong when you were always right." I gasped through tears and said again, "I'll never find anyone who loves me as much as you do."

She instantly held me in her arms with all her

warmth and familiar body scent. "You have acknowledged your mistake, and I am fine with that," she told me softly. "I hope you can now understand the consequences of rage."

I nodded and hugged her tighter. I listened carefully to her every word of advice, which I knew would be valuable in the future. Unlike before, her words no longer irritated me. Everything she said was for my own good.

The next six weeks were horrible. I was completely dependent on her, from brushing my teeth to getting into bed. She was always there to help me, no matter what, even with her own household chores to manage. She pampered me even more than she did for Sarah, and I felt ashamed of the mean feelings I had towards her before.

During my recovery, I had time to reflect Mom, who I used to find annoying, and I realized that she was actually the greatest blessing in my life. I felt grateful for her unwavering support and love, and I knew I could never thank her enough for all that she had done for me.

I finally understood why she wouldn't let Dad spend money on things like my videos - she loved him and knew how hard he worked for every rupee.

She scolded me when I wanted to indulge in junk food and play video games all day, not because she didn't love me, but because she wanted to take care of me and protect me. She wanted me to succeed in life, which is why she corrected me and worried about my studies.

I was her precious treasure, one she couldn't bear to lose. All this love and care was because she was my mom, the most wonderful creation of Allah, the Almighty.

Lets Have Fun!

Find The Words

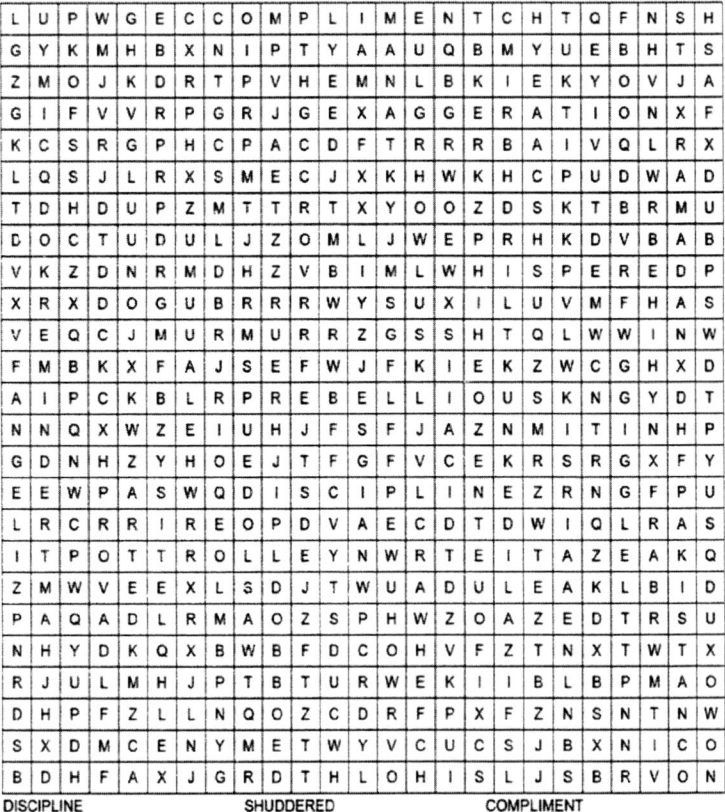

L	U	P	W	G	E	C	C	O	M	P	L	I	M	E	N	T	C	H	T	Q	F	N	S	H
G	Y	K	M	H	B	X	N	I	P	T	Y	A	A	U	Q	B	M	Y	U	E	B	H	T	S
Z	M	O	J	K	D	R	T	P	V	H	E	M	N	L	B	K	I	E	K	Y	O	V	J	A
G	I	F	V	V	R	P	G	R	J	G	E	X	A	G	G	E	R	A	T	I	O	N	X	F
K	C	S	R	G	P	H	C	P	A	C	D	F	T	R	R	R	B	A	I	V	Q	L	R	X
L	Q	S	J	L	R	X	S	M	E	C	J	X	K	H	W	K	H	C	P	U	D	W	A	D
T	D	H	D	U	P	Z	M	T	T	R	T	X	Y	O	O	Z	D	S	K	T	B	R	M	U
D	O	C	T	U	D	U	L	J	Z	O	M	L	J	W	E	P	R	H	K	D	V	B	A	B
V	K	Z	D	N	R	M	D	H	Z	V	B	I	M	L	W	H	I	S	P	E	R	E	D	P
X	R	X	D	O	G	U	B	R	R	R	W	Y	S	U	X	I	L	U	V	M	F	H	A	S
V	E	Q	C	J	M	U	R	M	U	R	R	Z	G	S	S	H	T	Q	L	W	W	I	N	W
F	M	B	K	X	F	A	J	S	E	F	W	J	F	K	I	E	K	Z	W	C	G	H	X	D
A	I	P	C	K	B	L	R	P	R	E	B	E	L	L	I	O	U	S	K	N	G	Y	D	T
N	N	Q	X	W	Z	E	I	U	H	J	F	S	F	J	A	Z	N	M	I	T	I	N	H	P
G	D	N	H	Z	Y	H	O	E	J	T	F	G	F	V	C	E	K	R	S	R	G	X	F	Y
E	E	W	P	A	S	W	Q	D	I	S	C	I	P	L	I	N	E	Z	R	N	G	F	P	U
L	R	C	R	R	I	R	E	O	P	D	V	A	E	C	D	T	D	W	I	Q	L	R	A	S
I	T	P	O	T	T	R	O	L	L	E	Y	N	W	R	T	E	I	T	A	Z	E	A	K	Q
Z	M	W	V	E	E	X	L	S	D	J	T	W	U	A	D	U	L	E	A	K	L	B	I	D
P	A	Q	A	D	L	R	M	A	O	Z	S	P	H	W	Z	O	A	Z	E	D	T	R	S	U
N	H	Y	D	K	Q	X	B	W	B	F	D	C	O	H	V	F	Z	T	N	X	T	W	T	X
R	J	U	L	M	H	J	P	T	B	T	U	R	W	E	K	I	I	B	L	B	P	M	A	O
D	H	P	F	Z	L	L	N	Q	O	Z	C	D	R	F	P	X	F	Z	N	S	N	T	N	W
S	X	D	M	C	E	N	Y	M	E	T	W	Y	V	C	U	C	S	J	B	X	N	I	C	O
B	D	H	F	A	X	J	G	R	D	T	H	L	O	H	I	S	L	J	S	B	R	V	O	N

DISCIPLINE SHUDDERED COMPLIMENT
ANGEL PERMISSION CHATTERING
TROLLEY EXTRACT WORSHIPER
PRAYERS MUSEUM RAMADAN
RUMMAGE REBELLIOUS CROWDED
PAKISTAN EXAGGERATION PIZZA
WHISPERED GIGGLE MURMUR
REVOLTING REMINDER

This is my favorite sketch from the story...

Choose your favorite moment from the story and sketch.

Do You Ride Bicycle Or A Hover Board?

Write Safety Instructions to ride a bicycle or a hoverboard.

-
-
-
-
-
-
-
-
-
-
-
-
-

It's time to write a book review.

Follow this step by step guide to write a wonderful review.

Step 1: Read the Book!

- Read the book from start to finish
- Take your time and enjoy the story

Step 2: Think About the Book

- What did you like about the book?

_____
_____
_____
_____
_____

- What you didn't like?

_____
_____
_____
_____
_____

- Who was your favorite character? and why?

_____
_____

- What was your favorite part in the book?

_____
_____
_____
_____

Step 3: Write Your Review in your note book.

- Start by writing the title of the book and the author's name

- Write a short summary of the story (1-2 paragraphs)

- Share your thoughts and opinions about the book (2-3 paragraphs)

- Use words like "I liked...", "I didn't like...", "My favorite part was...", etc.

- Be honest and have fun!

Step 4: Add Some Extras (Optional)

- Draw a picture of your favorite character or scene

- Write a poem or song lyrics inspired by the book

- Give the book a rating (e.g. 1-5 stars)

Step 5: Edit and Share!

- Read over your review to make sure it makes sense

- Ask a grown-up to help you edit if needed

- Share your review with friends, family, or even online!

Remember, the most important thing is to have fun and share your thoughts about the book!

Spot thirteen differences

About the Author:
Tayyaba Amir is a talented writer with a passion for storytelling and a deep love for literature. Born and raised in Pakistan, she draws inspiration from her diverse background to create rich and captivating narratives.

Writing Journey:
Tayyaba Amir's writing journey began at a young age when she discovered the power of words and their ability to transport readers to different worlds. As a child, she would spend hours lost in books, exploring the imaginations of beloved authors. During these formative years, she realised her desire to create stories that would captivate and inspire others. However, she started giving these stories a home by publishing in 2019.

Inspiration for the Book:
The inspiration for her book My Annoying Mom came from Tayyaba Amir's personal experiences and observations of mother-children relationships. With a keen eye for detail and a deep empathy for her characters, she delves into the complexities of relationships, personal growth, and overcoming adversity. Drawing on her journey of self-discovery, she weaves a compelling narrative that invites readers to reflect on their own lives.

Other Works:
In addition to her current book of the series, Amir has written several other remarkable works, each exploring different aspects of the young adults' experience. My Annoying Mom 2 is loved by the readers. Her novel, "The Chronicles of Deosai," gained a lot of fame internationally. Another remarkable work is "A Crescent and a Star" that's a must read for every Pakistani child to take inspiration from our unsung heroes. And for young readers, her picture book "Marium Wants to be a Princess" is indeed a joy.

Connect with the Author:
Stay connected with Tayyaba Amir on social media, where she shares her writing process, insights, and updates. Follow her on Facebook https://www.facebook.com/AuthorTayyabaAmir/ and Instagram @blissfulbutterflies1 to learn more about her books and upcoming projects.

Thank You:
Tayyaba Amir expresses her deepest gratitude to her readers for their unwavering support and for embarking on this literary journey with her. Their enthusiasm and encouragement continue to fuel her creativity and propel her to create meaningful and impactful stories. Without their steadfast presence, her writing would not be possible.